IF I MET AN ICE AGE ANIMAL

IF I SKATED WITH SABER-TOOTHED CATS

by Jenna Lee Gleisner
illustrated by Michelle Simpson

GRASSHOPPER

Tools for Parents & Teachers

Grasshopper Books enhance imagination and introduce the earliest readers to fiction with fun storylines and illustrations. The easy-to-read text supports early reading experiences with repetitive sentence patterns and sight words.

Before Reading

- Discuss the cover illustration. What do readers see?
- Look at the picture glossary together. Discuss the words.

Read the Book

- Read the book to the child, or have him or her read independently.
- "Walk" through the book and look at the illustrations. Who is the main character? What is happening in the story?

After Reading

- Prompt the child to think more. Ask: The main character imagines playing hockey with saber-toothed cats. If you could play a sport with any animal, what would it be? Why?

Grasshopper Books are published by Jump!
5357 Penn Avenue South
Minneapolis, MN 55419
www.jumplibrary.com

Library of Congress Cataloging-in-Publication Data

Names: Gleisner, Jenna Lee, author.
Simpson, Michelle (Illustrator), illustrator.
Title: If I skated with saber-toothed cats /
by Jenna Lee Gleisner; illustrated by Michelle Simpson.
Description: Minneapolis, MN: Jump!, Inc., 2023.
Series: If I met an Ice Age animal | Includes index.
Audience: Ages 5-8.
Identifiers: LCCN 2021060748 (print)
LCCN 2021060749 (ebook)
ISBN 9781636909516 (hardcover)
ISBN 9781636909523 (paperback)
ISBN 9781636909530 (ebook)
Subjects: CYAC: Saber-toothed tigers–Fiction.
Prehistoric animals–Fiction. | LCGFT: Picture books.
Classification: LCC PZ7.1.G5885 Ifm 2023 (print)
LCC PZ7.1.G5885 (ebook)
DDC [E]–dc23
LC record available at https://lccn.loc.gov/2021060748
LC ebook record available at https://lccn.loc.gov/2021060749

Editor: Eliza Leahy
Direction and Layout: Anna Peterson
Illustrator: Michelle Simpson

Printed in the United States of America at
Corporate Graphics in North Mankato, Minnesota.

Table of Contents

Big Teeth and Claws

Today, my hockey team is playing the Saber Tooths. I skate really fast!

What if I skated with real *saber-toothed cats?* I wonder.

Saber-toothed cats lived during the Ice Age. Everything was covered in ice and snow. That's OK! I'm used to skating outside in winter. I have all the gear I need to keep warm.

Saber tooths were large mammals. They had thick fur to keep warm.

They were big and strong.
One of the cats plays goalie.
He guards the net!

Saber-toothed cats had long claws. They could grip the ice.

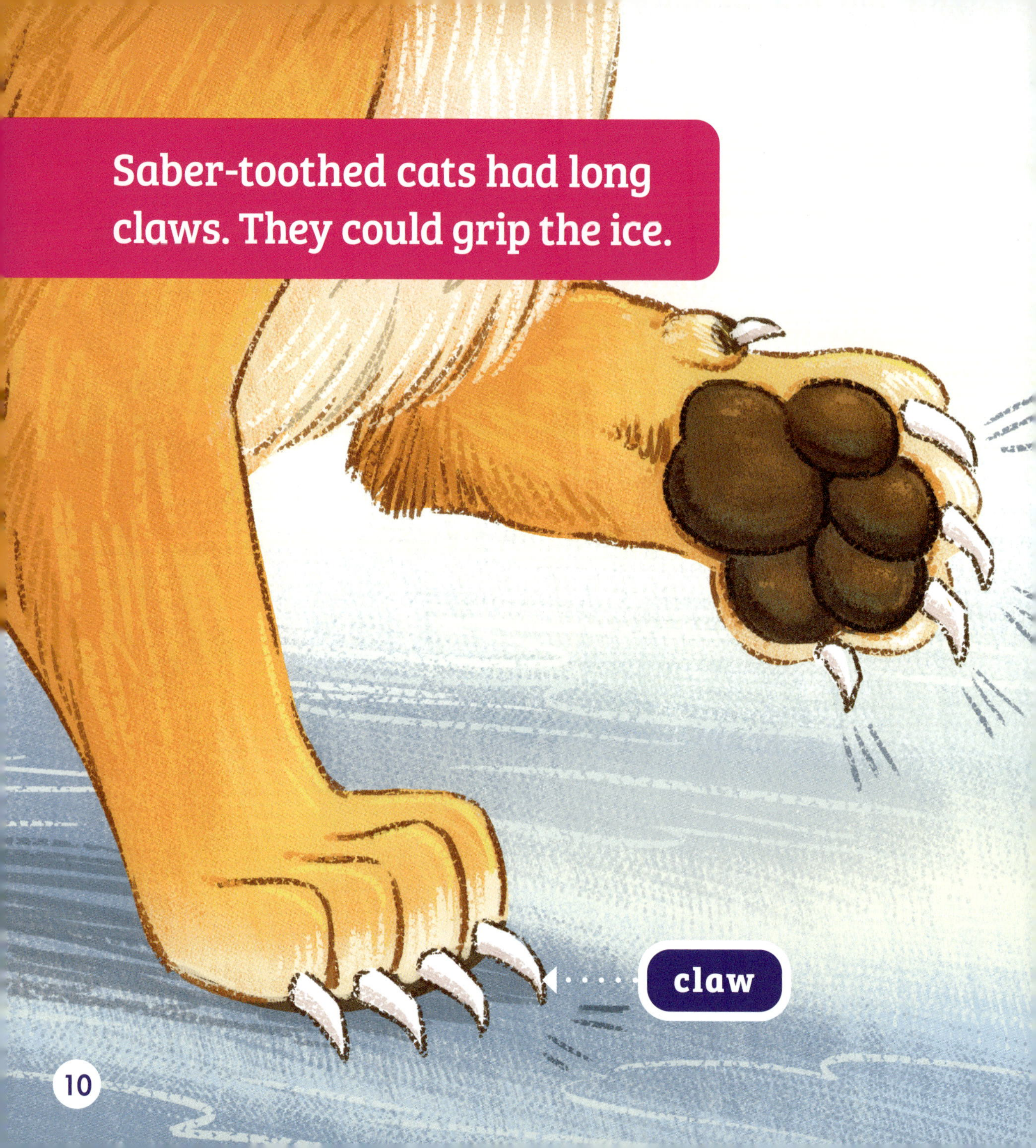

Saber tooths could chase after me, but I can skate faster!

Saber-toothed cats walked on all four legs. They wouldn't be able to hold hockey sticks. But they could use their saber-like teeth.

One of them stops the puck!

Saber tooths lived in packs.
A pack could make up a whole hockey team.

One cat passes the puck.
The pack cheers. They roar loudly!

Just then, there is a big crashing sound. A woolly mammoth walks through the forest.

The saber tooths stop skating. They are carnivores. They hunt woolly mammoths.

Just as one cat is about to slash the mammoth with its giant teeth, I hear a buzzer.

Buzz!

My team wins!

Good thing real saber tooths went extinct 10,000 years ago! I think as I shake hands with the Saber Tooths.

3
5

Parts of a Saber-Toothed Cat

Saber-toothed cats weighed more than 600 pounds (272 kilograms). They were almost six feet (1.8 meters) long. Take a look at the parts of a saber-toothed cat.

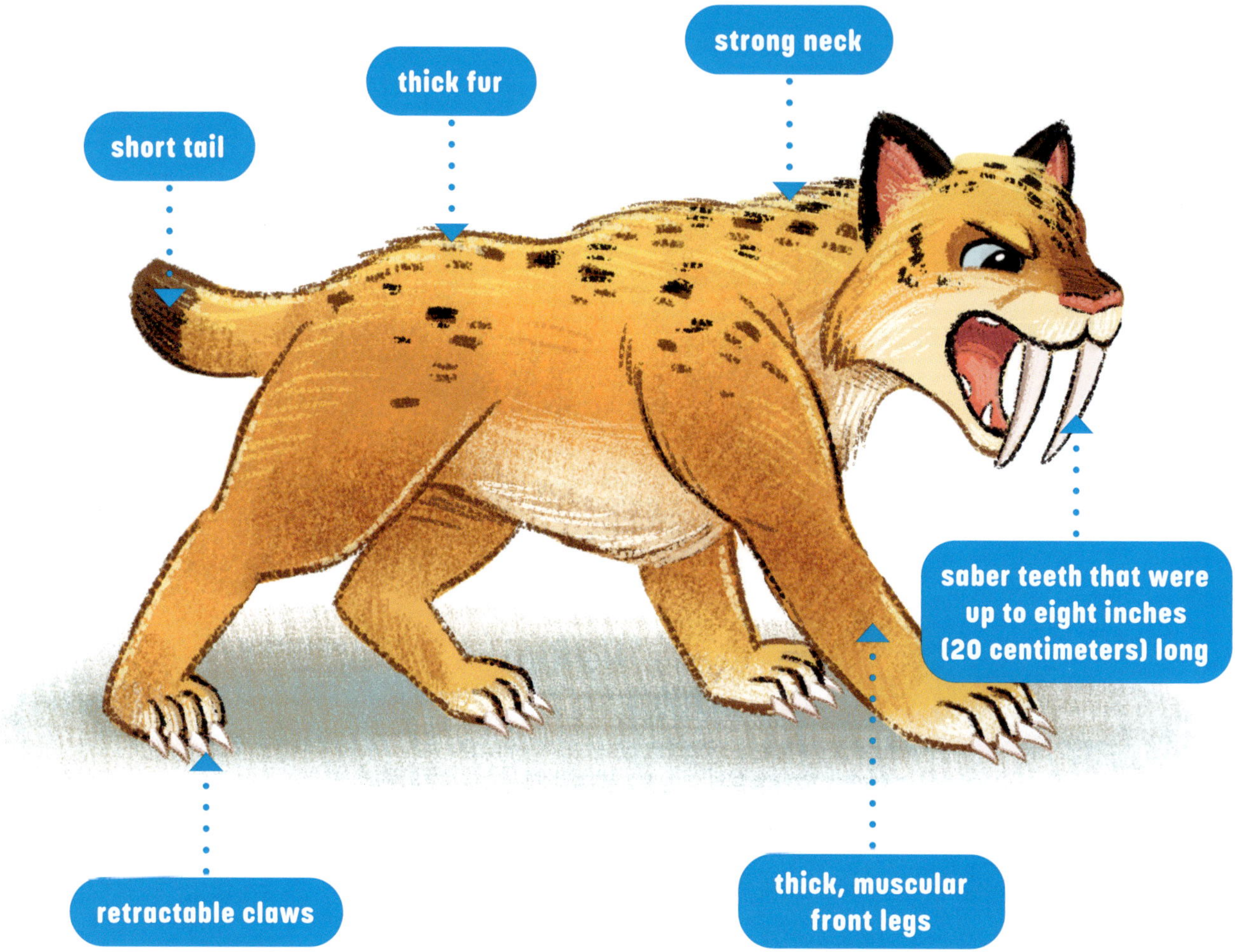

Picture Glossary

carnivores
Animals that eat meat.

extinct
No longer found alive and known about only through fossils or history.

Ice Age
A period of time, about 10,000 years ago, when a large part of Earth was covered with ice.

mammals
Warm-blooded animals with fur that usually give birth to live babies.

packs
Groups of saber-toothed cats.

saber
A large sword with a curved blade.

Index

To Learn More

FACT SURFER

Finding more information is as easy as 1, 2, 3.

1. Go to www.factsurfer.com
2. Enter "**ifIskatedwithsaber-toothedcats**" into the search box.
3. Choose your book to see a list of websites.